David Cole

History of Rockland County, New York

With Biographical Sketches of its Prominent Men

David Cole

History of Rockland County, New York
With Biographical Sketches of its Prominent Men

ISBN/EAN: 9783337241926

Printed in Europe, USA, Canada, Australia, Japan

Cover: Foto ©Raphael Reischuk / pixelio.de

More available books at **www.hansebooks.com**

NEW YORK,

—— WITH ——

BIOGRAPHICAL SKETCHES OF ITS PROMINENT MEN.

—— EDITED BY ——

REV. DAVID COLE. D. D.

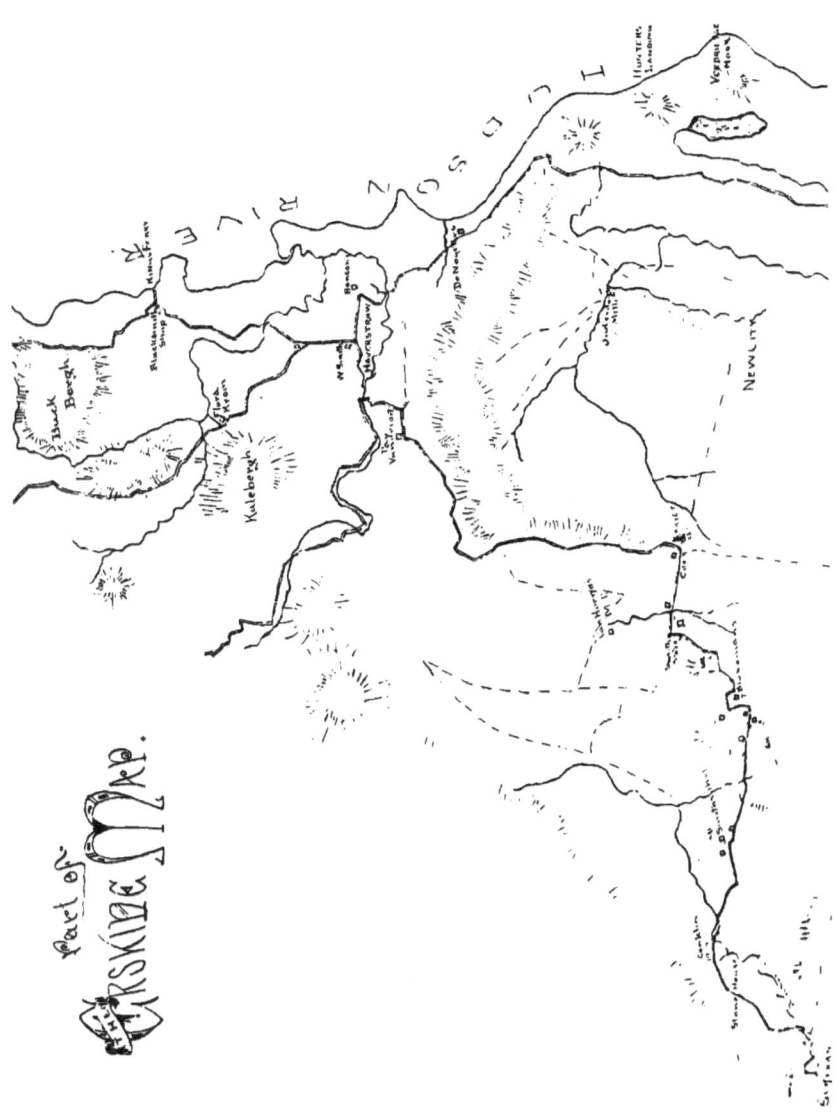

Part of

ERSKINE MAP.

PLAN OF
ROCKLAND CO.
NEW YORK.
Scale 2¼ miles to the inch.

James J. Stephens, M.D.

David Pye

ROSE HERMITAGE.

GEORGE D MACDOUGALL

Isaac Vanderbilt

Christian Dietzsch

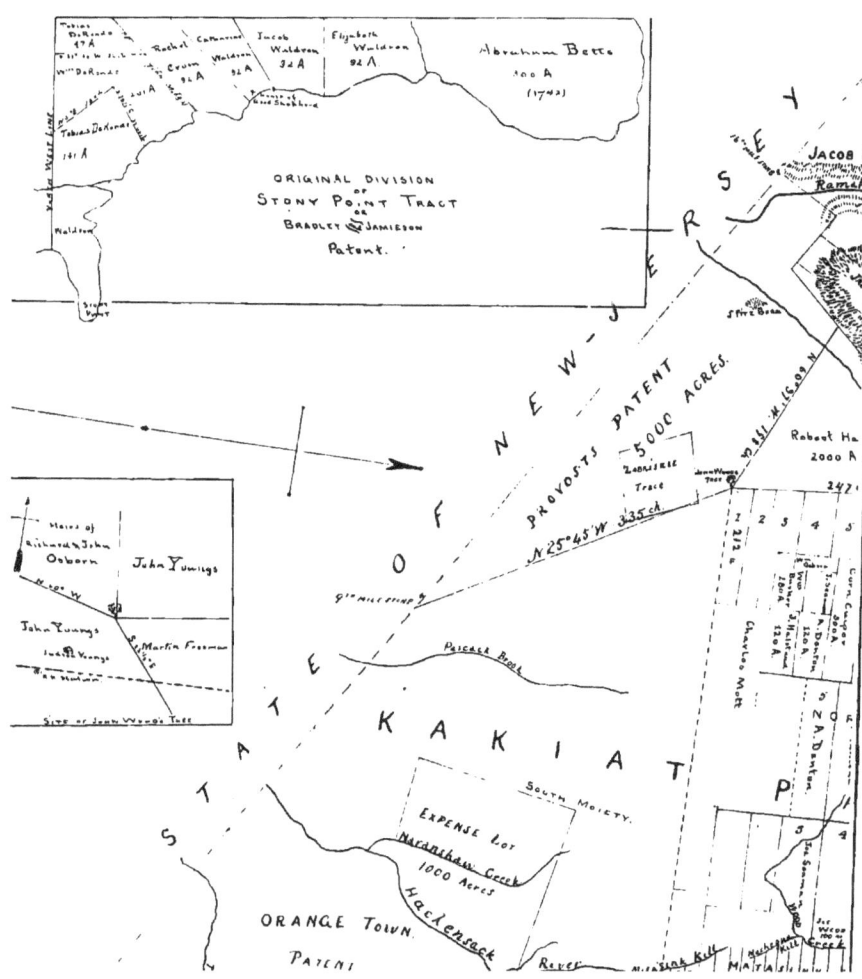

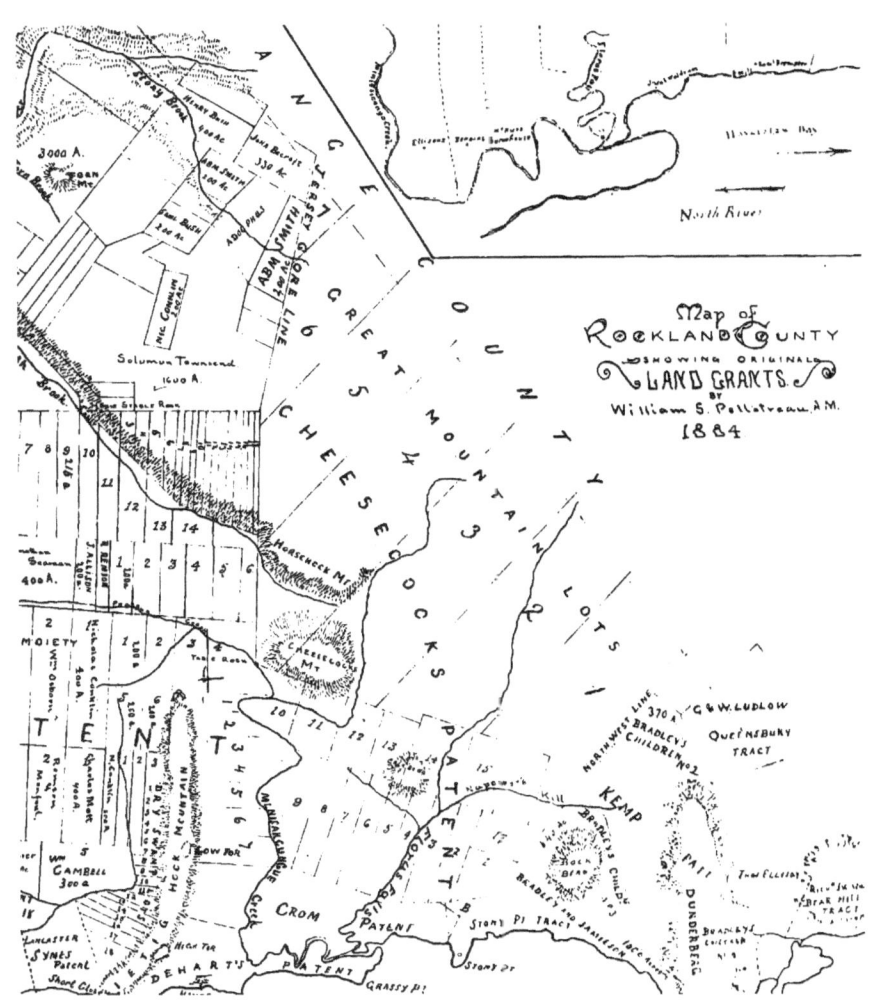

Map of
ROCKLAND COUNTY
SHOWING ORIGINAL
LAND GRANTS
BY
William S. Pelletreau, A.M.
1884

John W. Keller

Residence of JAMES E. WEST.

HOMESTEAD OF JOSEPH B ALLISON.
BUILT 1760.

BENJAMIN ALLISON.
Built 1754.

RELICS OF OLD HAVERSTRAW

J. J. McMahon

Residence of the Late JOHN PECK.

Amasa S. Freeman

Residence of JAMES GARNER WEST.

ROCKLAND COUNTY, N. Y.

Daniel. R. Wood

JAMES WOOD.

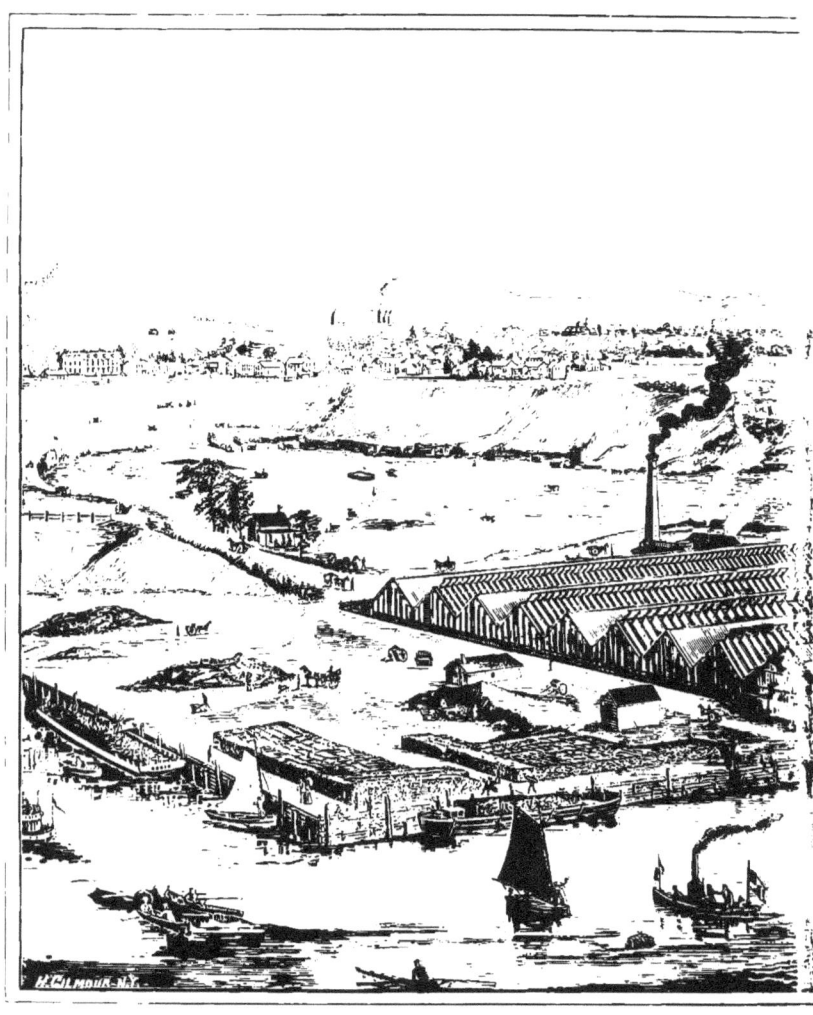

HN DERBYSHIRE.
A W.

George Knapp.

R. A. Ver Valen

John D. Norris

Very Respectfully
John Dobeer

J. C. Polhemus M. D.

REFORMED DUTCH CHURCH.

Piermont, N. Y.

Built 1836.

DUTCH REFORMED CHURCH,   TAPPAN.

AS RE-BUILT IN 1835.

DUTCH REFORMED CHURCH.
BUILT 1716.
WHERE MAJOR JOHN ANDRE
...
TAPPAN, N.Y.

PRESENT DUTCH REFORMED CHURCH,   TAPPAN

BUILT 1835

Isaac W. Cole

John W. Ferdon

William Voorhis

James D Blauvelt

Isaac J. Wistar

John B. Gardner

Jacob Snider

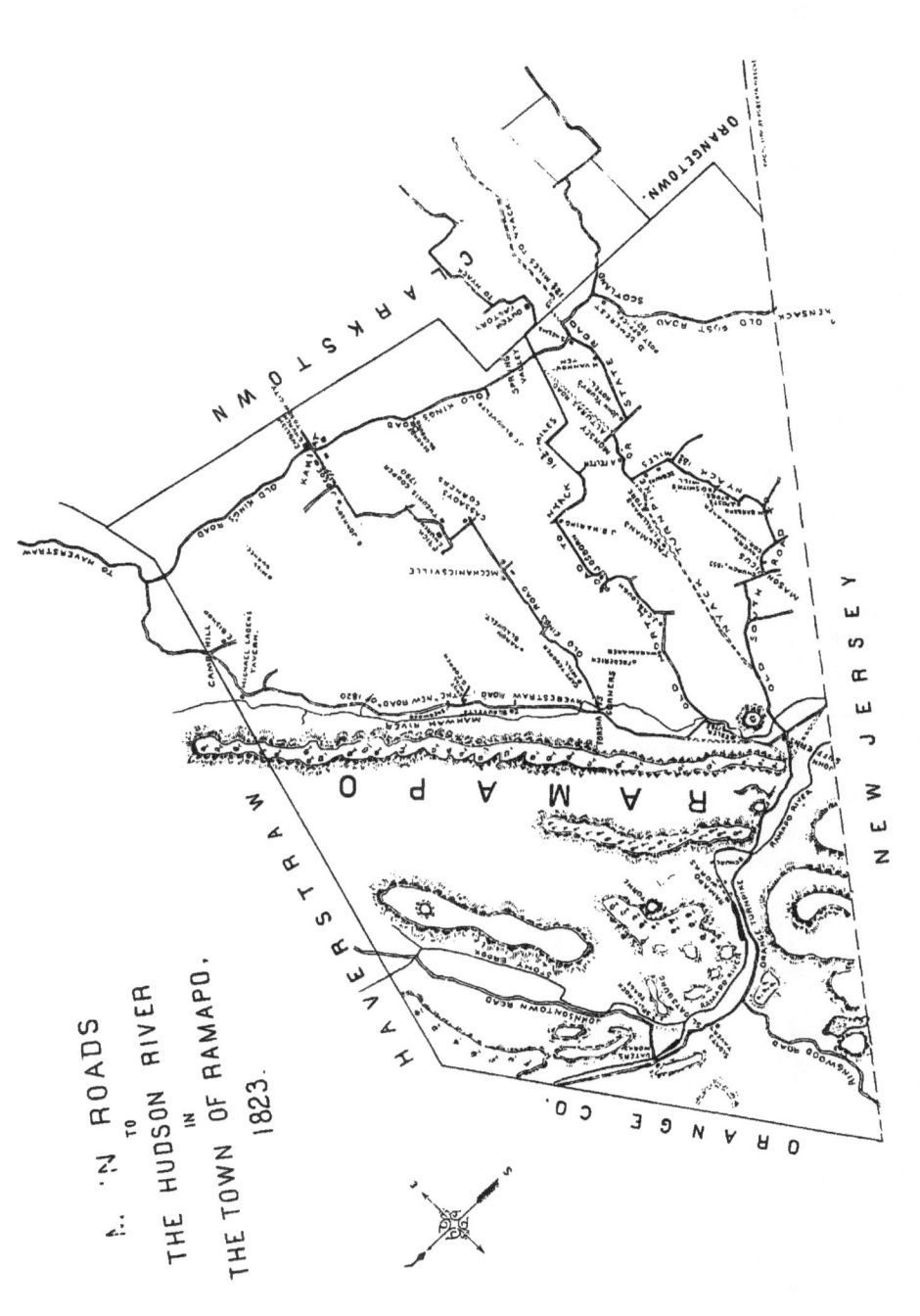

ROADS
TO
THE HUDSON RIVER
IN
THE TOWN OF RAMAPO.
1823.

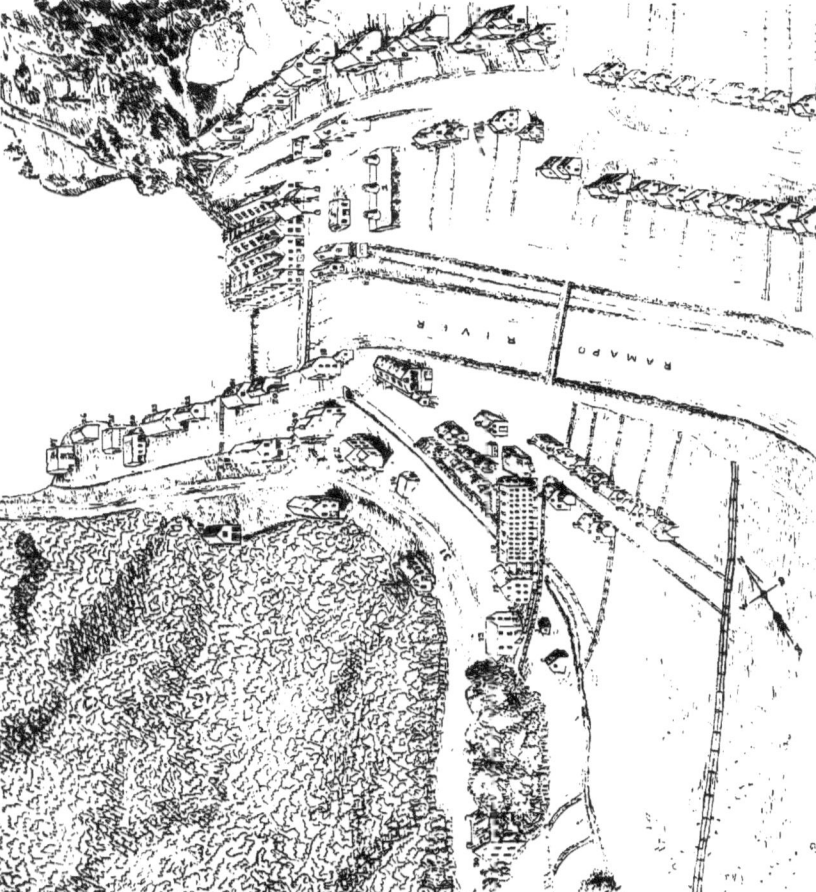

RAMAPO "IN YE OLDEN TIMES."

REFERENCES.

1. Nail Works, and Rolling Mill.
2. Steel Furnace.
3. Foundry.
4. Wheelwright Shop.
5. Pattern Shop.
6. Store Room and Hoe Factory.
7. Coal House.
8. Forge and Wire Works.
9. Smith Shop.
10. Cotton Mill.
11. Dye House.
12. Screw Factory and Machine Shop.
13. Store House.
14. Coal House.
15. School House.
16. Parsonage.
17. Store House.
18. Store.
19. Grist Mill.
20. Saw Mill.
21. Straw Mill.
22. Horse Stables.
23. Oxen and Mule Stables.
24. Mule Stables.
25. Barn and Slaughter House.
26. Barn.
27. Carriage House.
28. Pierson Family Mansion.
29. Pierson Family Mansion.
30. Old Road through "Pass" now
    Orange Turnpike.

The Village extended beyond the limits of this sketch, and included the church and burying grounds, and 19 dwellings not herein shown.

A. S. Zabriskie

VIEW OF STABLES & FISH POND FROM THE EAST.

James Shurwood

Erastus Johnson

Daniel Johnson

George Concklin

خاک

Daniel Tompkins

Wilson Tomkins

William Bovens

SM

www.ingramcontent.com/pod-product-compliance
Lightning Source LLC
Chambersburg PA
CBHW020234030726
47497CB00009B/3083